© for the French edition: L'Élan vert, Saint-Pierre-des-Corps, 2019
Title of the original edition: Une Poupée pour Maman
© for the English edition: Prestel Verlag, Munich • London • New York, 2020
A member of Verlagsgruppe Random House GmbH
Neumarkter Strasse 28 • 81673 Munich

For the photos: Female statuette Akua'ba
13 x 4.7 x 2.1 inches (32.9 x 12 x 5.4 cm)
© Musée du Quai Branly-Jacques-Chirac,
Dist. RMN-Grand Palais / image Musée du Quai Branly-Jaques-Chirac.

Library of Congress Control Number: 2019953589
A CIP catalogue record for this book is available from the British Library.

Translated from the French by Paul Kelly
Copyediting: Brad Finger
Project management: Melanie Schöni
Production management and typesetting: Susanne Hermann
Printing and binding: TBB, a.s.

FSC MIX From responsible sources FSC® C022120

Verlagsgruppe Random House FSC® N001967

Our production is climate neutral
ClimatePartner.com/14044-1912-1001
Print product

Prestel Publishing compensates the CO_2 emissions produced
from the making of this book by supporting a reforestation project
in Brazil. Find further information on the project here:
www.ClimatePartner.com/14044-1912-1001

Printed in Slovakia
ISBN 978-3-7913-7446-8
www.prestel.com

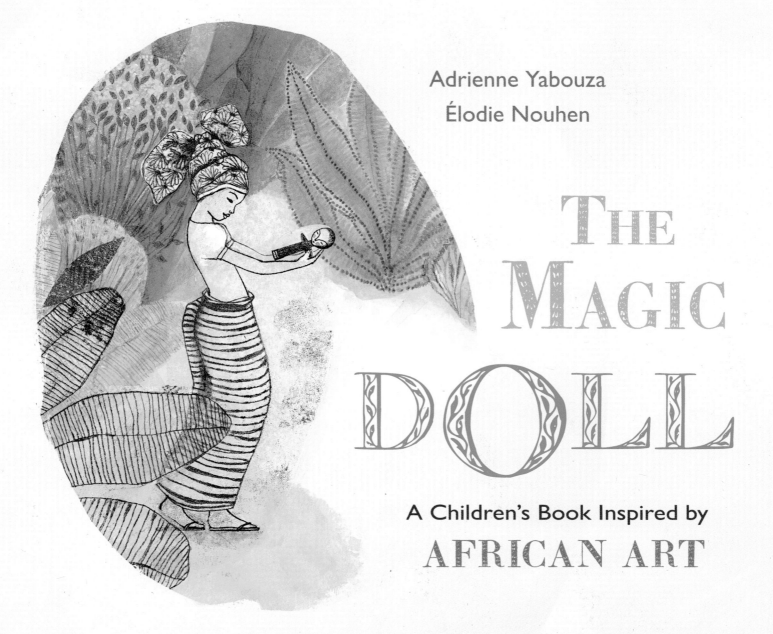

Adrienne Yabouza

Élodie Nouhen

THE MAGIC DOLL

A Children's Book Inspired by
AFRICAN ART

PRESTEL

Munich · London · New York

The sky is blue. Blue skies…

Against the blue, the sun looks like the yolk of an egg in a frying pan.

Today is just like every other day – it's scorching hot and my mom is preparing a meal.

She is in the kitchen, outside. But I am not the only one watching what she is doing.

Mom has placed her doll, named Dolly, not far away. It lies at the foot of the mango tree that offers shade for our yard. The doll's real name is Akua'ba, but mom and I prefer Dolly because it just sounds right.

This beautiful Dolly, ever so wise, is my big sister. She was born one year before me, and I know that because mom told me so.

One day, mom got married.
There was a celebration where
everyone wore pretty cloth garments.
Oh, such beautiful colors!
And then came the day after the wedding,
and then the next day,
and the days after that…
and time slipped by.

The rainy season followed
the dry season, and then
another rainy season came.
All throughout this time, mom
was checking her belly. Flat!
Her friends who had married
around the same time all had
round stomachs! Some of them
were as round as a big balloon.
All of the parents, neighbors,
and friends were saying to
mom, "Ama, when are you
going to have your baby?"
"Ama, is your first baby
going to be a boy or a girl?"
"Ama, are you waiting for
the big season to have a child?
Or for the little season?"
Everyone laughed.
Nobody was aware, however,
that mom would cry in the evening.

This is Kwame. He married my mom and
loves her very much. One day, he suggested,
"If you want to, please go and see a carver.
He will make you a doll, a pretty one that
you can carry. After that we may have a child."
Mom went and got her doll.
Now she carries it on her back.

In the morning, after taking a shower
in the big bowl, mom rolled up her doll
in its double loincloth and wore Dolly
on her back, as one carries a child.
When mom went to the market
to buy rice, or millet, or yams,
or something else, she always took
her doll along with her…
When mom was preparing fish,
or dough, or the sauce, she would
always keep the doll on her back.

Time went by. Another rainy season was
followed by another dry season.
And then yet another rainy season came.
All the while, no matter whether the sky
was blue, gray, or dark, mom would look
at her belly. She touched it with her hand.

Every day, she would talk to the doll.
"Please give me a child, Dolly!
If you make my belly round,
I will kiss you a thousand times
on your eyes and on your nose.
Dolly! On a bright sunlit day or a clear
moonlit night, please give me a child."

Time passed by a little bit more, and then
what was meant to arrive finally did!
It was on an evening or a morning, or perhaps
it was in the middle of the day or the night.
Mom touched her belly and sensed it was different,
maybe a little rounder. She touched it again and again.
And then she kissed the doll, which was sitting there
and watching her.
She called to Kwame, and he came over.
"My husband, sit down," she said.
"But Ama, why?," he asked.
"Take a seat and listen."
She told him the news. And having waited so long, he hugged his wife.

After a moment, and in a thoughtful manner, he said,

"Let's keep this news to ourselves. It is our secret.

Let us wait a bit for someone to notice

your round belly."

A little more time passed by, and then what was meant
to happen actually happened.
It was a neighbor who took notice and asked,
"Ama, is what I am seeing with my eyes true? Is your belly round?
Are you expecting a baby?"
Ama replied as if it were not important. "But every woman carries
her baby in her belly before carrying it on her back, doesn't she?"
Words do not have legs, but sometimes they can run fast!
An hour later, the whole village had learned of Ama's joy.
The news may even have spread to the big city of Koumassi.

Mom would take care of her doll every day.

One day, she dressed it in a necklace of pearls.

On another day, she forgot the pearls
and put an earring on it instead.

Mom did not know it yet, but this was me,
Adjoa, in her belly.

I was waiting. I was waiting for my day. . .

And then I was born.
With a smile, mom asked my father,
"Which one will I love the most? Your daughter or my doll?"
"You, Ama, and I, Kwame, we have two hearts. There is
enough between us to love both Adjoa, our daughter, and the doll."
Mom smiled, which is more than the doll did because it
always looked very serious.

The sky is blue. It is a blue sky.
And in the blue of the sky, the sun looks
like the yolk of an egg in a frying pan.
Today is just like every day — it is hot
and my mom is preparing a meal.
I look at her and see that her belly
is round again, just like a balloon.

Female statuette

AKUA'BA

Statuette of fertility and protection
for pregnant women.
Made in Ghana by the Ashanti tribe,

in wood and pearls.
13 x 4.7 x 2.1 inches (32.9 x 12 x 5.4 cm)
Museum du Quai Branly-Jacques-Chirac, Paris.

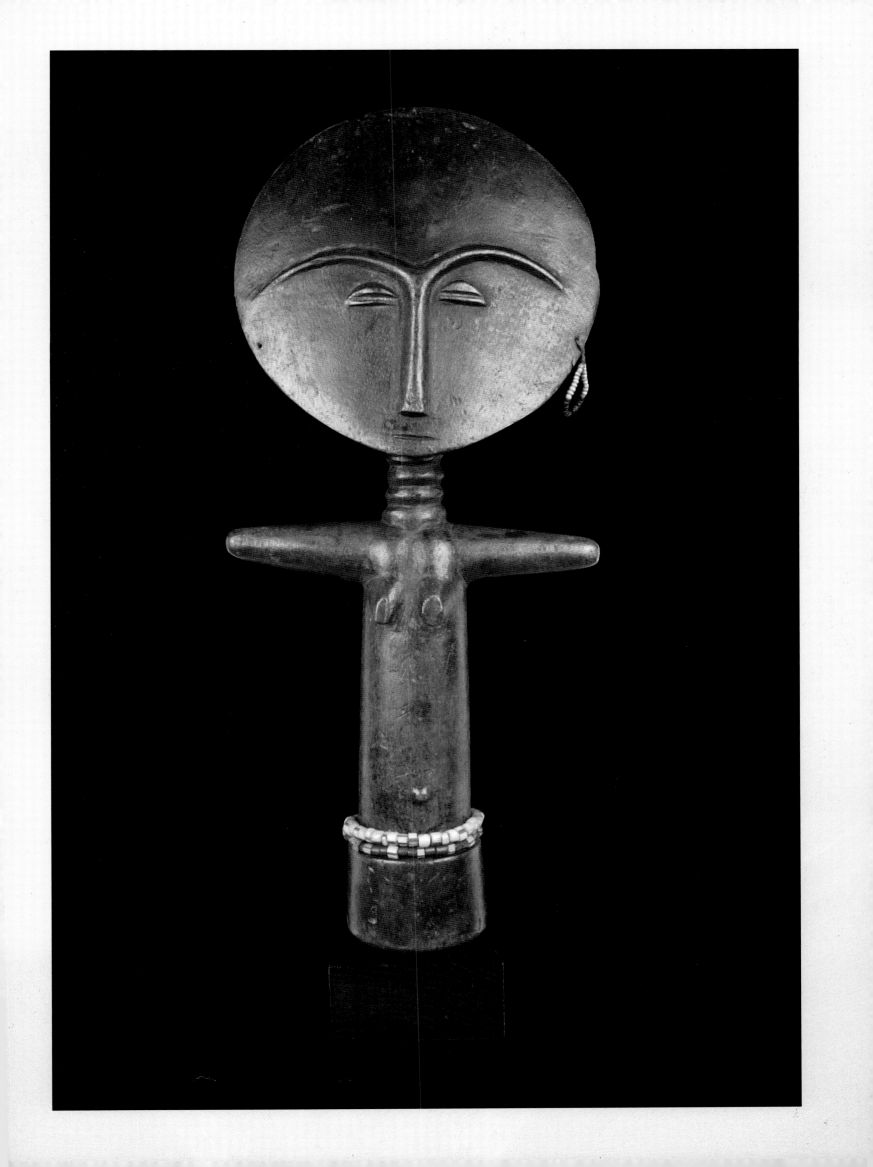

THE AKUA'BA DOLL

Africa or the Africas?

It is difficult to talk about a single Africa. More than 50 countries make up this huge continent. There are dry regions and heavily flooded ones; regions with great rivers and big trees and areas of broad savannah; rainforest expanses and vast deserts. And that's not all! We're talking about a continent where over a thousand languages are spoken and where multiple religions from around the world have spread and often replaced traditional beliefs. A place with such diversity should not be called 'Africa,' it should be called the Africas! African peoples have a long history of great empires and artistic talent. Archaeology has discovered traces of paintings and of the use of bones as tools from thousands of years ago. An ancient text tells us of three great empires at the beginning of the 2nd century: the Romans, the Persians, and the Kingdom of Aksum. This last kingdom, from present-day Ethiopia, was famous for its large obelisks, each of which were fashioned from one huge slab of granite. Ten books would not be enough to write about the great Zimbabwe, the princes of Mali, and the kingdoms of Benin. The Africas contained artists working with leather, wood, metal, etc. There were craftspeople who wove canvases to decorate with paint. Other artists created music and invented poems that became songs. And just as no hunter would kill game other than for food, no artist would speak, carve, or compose merely for fun. Art was meant to have a social function; to heal or celebrate an individual person or a society.

The Dolls

Dolls are widespread in Africa. They are common among all communities and in a range of materials from cloth to pearls. The best-known African dolls, however, are typically made of carved wood. The Ibeji twin dolls in the Yoruba country, the Nyeleni doll from the Bambara people of Mali, and the Biga doll from the Mossi of Burkina Faso are especially eye-catching. The purpose of the latter two is to allow women to become fertile and help them get pregnant. We could also single out the beautiful doll figurines made by the Fang people in Central Africa or the Senufo in Western Africa.

Akua'ba (Akwaba), the Ashanti Doll

As is often the case, truth becomes myth. In the Ashanti language, *Akua* is supposed to mean 'born on Wednesday' and *ba* means 'child.' Legend has it that a bride called Akua was unable to have a child. So she was advised to carve a doll out of wood and to wear it on her back, treasuring it as her own offspring. People in the village mocked her, but the following year she gave birth to a pretty little girl! Today, as in earlier times, many women in the Ashanti communities do as Akua did with her doll to ensure they will become pregnant and that they will give birth without problems.

Akua'bas are certainly among the most beautiful carved dolls. Some types are carried by women who want to have a girl, while others are carried by women desiring a boy. All of them, however, have an almost cylindrical body and a disc-shaped face. Ashanti women also wear gold or silver pendants that bear the image of a fertility doll.